BRIELLE'S BIRTHDAY BALL

ONCE UPON A
Dance

ILLUSTRATED BY STELLA MONGODI

Dedicated
to anyone
who loves
a good
dance party!

Brielle's Birthday Ball
A Dance-It-Out Creative Movement Story for Young Movers

© 2021 *Once Upon a Dance*
Illustrated and cover design by Stella Mongodi, www.stellamarisart.it
Layout in collaboration with Carla Green, Clarity Designworks

All 2021 book sales donated to ballet companies struggling under COVID-19.

Each Dance-It-Out story is an independent kids' dance performance ready for the imagination stage. In this volume, readers travel along with Brielle on her birthday journey to the moon. Ballerina Konora provides movement motivation and helps readers connect with storytelling, focus their breath, and explore dance fundamentals.

Library of Congress Control Number: 2021910130
ISBN 978-1-955555-00-5 (paperback); 978-1-955555-01-2 (ebook); 978-1-955555-02-9 (hardcover)
Juvenile Fiction: Bedtime & Dreams
(Juvenile Fiction: Imagination & Play; Juvenile Fiction: Holidays & Celebrations: Birthdays; Juvenile Fiction: Performing Arts: Dance; Juvenile Fiction: Science Fiction: Space Exploration)

First Edition

Other *Once Upon a Dance* Titles:
Joey Finds His Jump!: A Dance-It-Out Creative Movement Story for Young Movers
Petunia Perks Up: A Dance-It-Out Movement and Meditation Story
Danny, Denny, and the Dancing Dragon: A Dance-It-Out Creative Movement Story for Young Movers
Princess Naomi Helps a Unicorn: A Dance-It-Out Creative Movement Story for Young Movers
The Cat with the Crooked Tail: A Dance-It-Out Creative Movement Story for Young Movers
Mira Monkey's Magic Mirror Adventure: A Dance-It-Out Creative Movement Story for Young Movers
Belluna's Adventure in the Sky: A Dance-It-Out Creative Movement Story for Young Movers
Dancing Shapes: Ballet and Body Awareness for Young Dancers
More Dancing Shapes: Ballet and Body Awareness for Young Dancers
Nutcracker Dancing Shapes: Shapes and Stories from Konora's Twenty-Five Nutcracker Roles
Dancing Shapes with Attitude: Ballet and Body Awareness for Young Dancers
Konora's Shapes: Poses from Dancing Shapes for Creative Movement & Ballet Teachers
More Konora's Shapes: Poses from More Dancing Shapes for Creative Movement & Ballet Teachers
Ballerina Dreams Ballet Inspiration Journal/Notebook
Dancing Shapes Ballet Inspiration Journal/Notebook

Hello Fellow Dancer,

My name is Ballerina Konora. I love stories, adventures, and ballet.

I'm glad you're here with me! Will you be my dance partner and act out this story with me and Brielle? I've included descriptions of movements that express the story. You can decide whether to use these ideas or create your own moves. Be safe, of course, and do what works for your body in your space. And if you'd rather just settle in and enjoy the pictures the first time through, that's fine, too.

Konora

P.S. Boy or girl, you can move like all the characters and objects in this story.

Once upon a dance, Brielle twirled about in excitement. She had been counting the days to her birthday, and now, at last, it was almost here. On the day she was born, she was brand new. Now, she slept in her own bed and was learning to write words, add numbers, draw, and paint.

Tomorrow was the big day! She would eat birthday cake and ice cream, and open presents. She could hardly wait!

Will you join me in my *I'm-excited* dance? We clap our hands together and rub them back and forth as quickly as we can. Then we stretch our arms up in a big V and reach our chests toward the ceiling. This usually makes me yawn. See if you can find a little yawn somewhere and let it out. Then, let that happy energy spin you around in a joyful twirl.

How does your body react to happy news?

Brielle put on her pajamas and brushed her teeth especially well. She was so excited, she wasn't sure she'd be able to fall asleep.

"The sooner you fall asleep, the sooner it will be tomorrow," her mother reminded her.

Brielle nodded, climbed into bed, and closed her eyes. She hoped to get up early so her special day would be as long as possible.

Let's pretend to put on our pajamas. Lift your foot extra high to put on the PJ pants: one foot, then the other. Reach your arms into the sleeves and give a little shimmy to get everything in place. Now it's time for our toothbrush and toothpaste. Let's sing a happy little song while we brush:

Brush it up, brush it down, brushing, brushing all around.
First in front, then in back, got to get rid of the plaque.
Tops and bottoms of the teeth. Oh, puh-leeze do not be brief.
Take your time, brush them well. And your smile will be swell!

It was dark and quiet in Brielle's room when she heard a noise outside her bedroom door.

Tiptoeing to the door, she pulled it open. On the floor was a package: FOR BRIELLE, HAPPY BIRTHDAY.

Brielle looked up and down the hall, but she didn't see anyone. She picked up the package and crept back into her room.

Brielle eyed the clock. 2:00 a.m. It was already her birthday!

Imagine cautiously opening your door and peeking out.

Reach your neck out and slowly look in both directions.

Pick up the present and quietly tiptoe back into your room.

Brielle set the package on her desk. Then she sat on her bed and looked at the gift.

Should I open it now? she wondered.

Something seemed to glow inside the paper.

I'll just take a little peek.

Let's pretend to gently set the package on our desk.

We do a backward scoot and press down with our hands to get up on the bed.

Elbows on the knees, hands on the chin, is one good thinking position.

Brielle peeled back the wrapping. Inside was a ball, but not an ordinary ball.

She took it out of the paper. *I am a magic birthday ball,* she read. *Yours until morning. Follow me for your birthday adventure. In the morning, we must both be back home.*

Suddenly, the ball, which reminded Brielle of a little moon, jumped out of her hands. It rolled out of her room and down the hall to the front door.

Pretend to unwrap the ball, then character switch-a-roo and pretend to *be* the ball. Onto the ground we go, and roll sideways. As the ball stops, find a moment of stillness and rest.

Brielle's mouth fell open in wonder. She put on her bathrobe and slippers, then followed the ball. It seemed to be waiting for her.

As she neared the ball, it began to knock against the door.

Brielle carefully picked the ball up again.

Whoosh! Like magic, she began to rise into the sky.

Let's act out putting on our bathrobe and slippers. Arms into the robe and crisscross our arms to close it. One foot at a time wiggles into a soft slipper. We walk to the door, turn the handle, and push it open.

Reach down to get your ball. Surprise! Act out your wonder at flying up into the air while holding on tight.

Up and up Brielle went, over buildings and parks, and all the way into space!

Brielle held the ball tight. She bounced off what looked like a cloud, even though clouds shouldn't be solid. She started bouncing from cloud to cloud, moving closer to the moon with each bounce.

Just as she wondered if she'd ever stop, she landed on top of a pile of soft balls that all looked like her birthday ball. The ball tugged her gently from the pile and set her lightly on the ground.

Do you want to gently flop into something soft? Maybe a couch or a bean bag? How about a carpet? Dancers practice carefully falling, not only as practice for dance moves, but to make sure we don't hurt ourselves if we accidentally fall. Keep your knees and elbows bent and think of shrinking yourself down before you flop.

17

While Brielle was looking around, the birthday ball jumped out of her hands and rolled away. Following it, Brielle spied a hole in the ground with a ladder sticking up out of it.

The ball dropped into the hole.

Brielle looked down. A soft glow filled the hole. Her ball was waiting for her.

Curious, Brielle climbed down.

Let's act out a little more ball rolling. Try squeezing yourself into a round shape with your knees to your chest, and roll sideways.

Then let's switch to Brielle climbing down the ladder—our hands move almost in circles as we pretend to move from one ladder rung to the one below it. Our feet feel like we're marching backward as we imagine climbing down one foot at a time. After my foot touches the ground, my knees bend and my bottom reaches out behind me.

19

Brielle reached the bottom and picked up her ball. At that moment, a bunch of little people jumped out and said, "Surprise! Happy Birthday!"

A band in a corner of the room started playing music, and all the people started to dance.

Let's pretend we're saying a surprise hello to Brielle. I think I might give a little jump in my excitement. How would you express your welcoming joy?

Brielle stood there with her mouth open in shock. A man and a woman who were a little taller than the others walked up to her. "Welcome to your birthday celebration dance party!" the man said as he stretched his arms up in a V.

"Thank you," said Brielle. "But . . . where am I, and who are you?"

"You're on the moon, of course," he said. "I'm the Man in the Moon, and these are my wife and children. They will help you celebrate becoming another year older."

Dance Party! Oh yeah, I can get into that. Do you have a favorite song? Now would be a good time to sing a bit and free-style dance in whatever way you like. Imagine you're one of lots of kids on the moon, dancing with your family. You could pretend you weigh less and feel lighter because gravity isn't as strong on the moon.

The Man in the Moon gave Brielle a hat that looked a lot like her birthday ball. Then he pointed to a fountain with what seemed to be blue water cascading down. Next to it was a table covered with cupcakes. On the other side was the biggest candle Brielle had ever seen.

And there, resting against the candle, was another ladder.

I think it would be fun—but a little tricky—to pretend to be a fountain: see if you can create the feeling of water flowing up and out and down with your movement. Then, let's pretend to be a nice round cupcake, either with just our arms or our whole bodies making a circle.

"Have fun at your birthday celebration, Brielle," the Man in the Moon said. "Dance, eat, drink, laugh. When you are ready to go home, just climb up the ladder and blow out the candle."

Brielle tasted a cupcake. Oh, was it good! She drank some of the blue water. It was minty and chocolatey at the same time.

Let's act out eating a cupcake! Lean forward a little and take a big bite. Yummy! Rub your tummy in a circle to show your appreciation and enjoyment.

Look at that blue water. How would you take a drink if you didn't know what something was? I think my face would look curious, and it would only be a small sip.

Brielle danced to the music. Around her, the Man in the Moon's children did donkey kicks and monkey jumps. They were having great fun.

Let's re-create those silly moves. To do a monkey jump, put your hands on the ground, lift both feet up, and scoot your legs a little sideways. If that works out alright, try to scoot them a little farther the next time.

For donkey kicks, same idea, but we throw our feet up a little higher in the air and don't do the scoot.

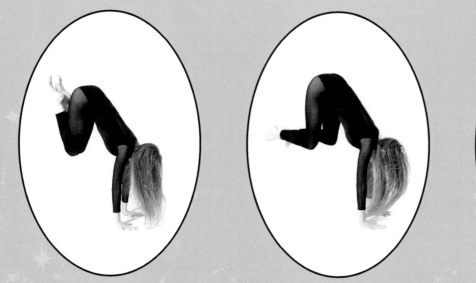

Brielle thought she would never want to leave. But after a while, she began to grow tired. She thought of her little bed at home, and how nice it would feel to lie down in it.

She thought it was, perhaps, time to go home.

Yum, another chance for a delicious yawn. Let's move our hand to our mouth and almost tap our hand to our lips a few times to let our bodies know it's time for a yawn. Then reach our arms up and back. Let your eyes look for the ceiling and take a big breath in.

Brielle thanked the Man in the Moon and his wife for the lovely party. She bowed as she said her goodbyes.

"I'm so happy you enjoyed yourself," said the Man in the Moon.

"You must come back some day," said his wife.

Brielle nodded. She would like that very much.

Brielle climbed the ladder. After one last look back, she turned and blew out the candle.

Imagine you're saying goodbye. Give a little curtsy or bow to your host.

Then let's be the moon family waving their goodbyes.

Now let's climb that ladder up, up, up. Reach above to the next rung, step up, and repeat. Keep your elbows to the side so they don't hit the ladder. Take a gigantic breath in, then blow out the candle through rounded lips.

Brielle opened her eyes. She was in her bed. It was morning. She could hear the birds singing.

Her mother and father were standing at the door. "Happy Birthday, Brielle," they said.

Brielle sat up and looked around. Her bathrobe and slippers were where they had been the night before. There was no paper. No magic ball.

It must have been a dream, she thought.

Imagine waking up in your bed. You slowly sit up and look all around. Maybe rub your eyes and give another delicious yawn and wiggle. Let your inner storyteller shine as you act out Brielle's surprise at finding herself back home, her wonder at her experience, and her confusion over whether it was all just a dream.

Thee end!
The end.

My grandpa always ended stories this way, and I like to share the fun.

Thank you for being my dance partner.

Until our next adventure,

Love,

Konora

WE'RE WAITING FOR YOUR FEEDBACK

We check for new reviews each day and would be immensely grateful for a kind, honest review at Amazon or Goodreads.

Brielle's Birthday Ball is a mother-daughter COVID-collaboration (and this story's based on grandma's story). We were both immersed in the ballet world until the pandemic, and it took a lot of learning to publish this book. We really hope you like it and tell your friends who might enjoy it.

Made in the USA
Las Vegas, NV
13 September 2022